FGHIJK

QRSTU

ABCDE

LMNOP

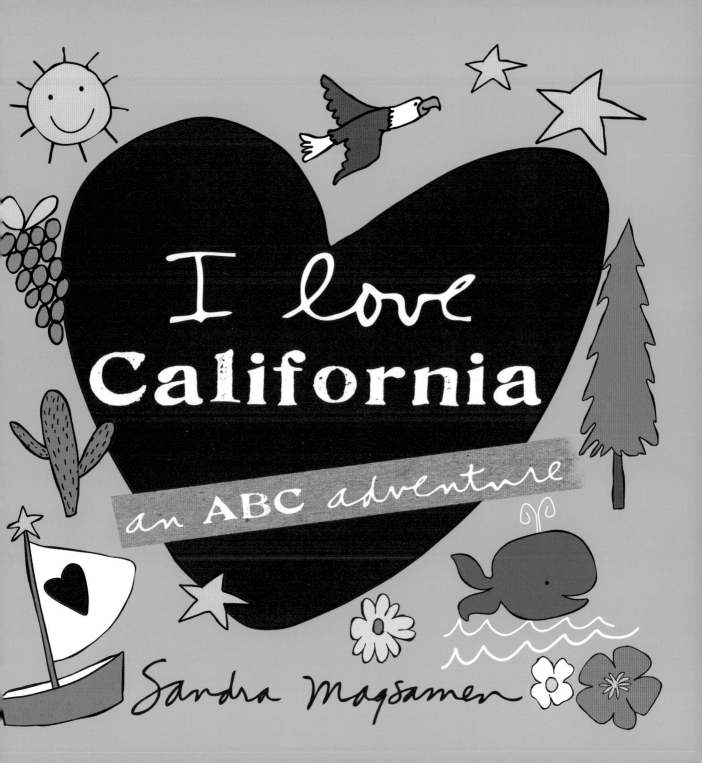

I love California

an ABC adventure

Sandra Magsamen

California is filled with fantastic and beautiful things to see and do. Just follow the **A, B, C's,** there is an amazing adventure waiting for you!

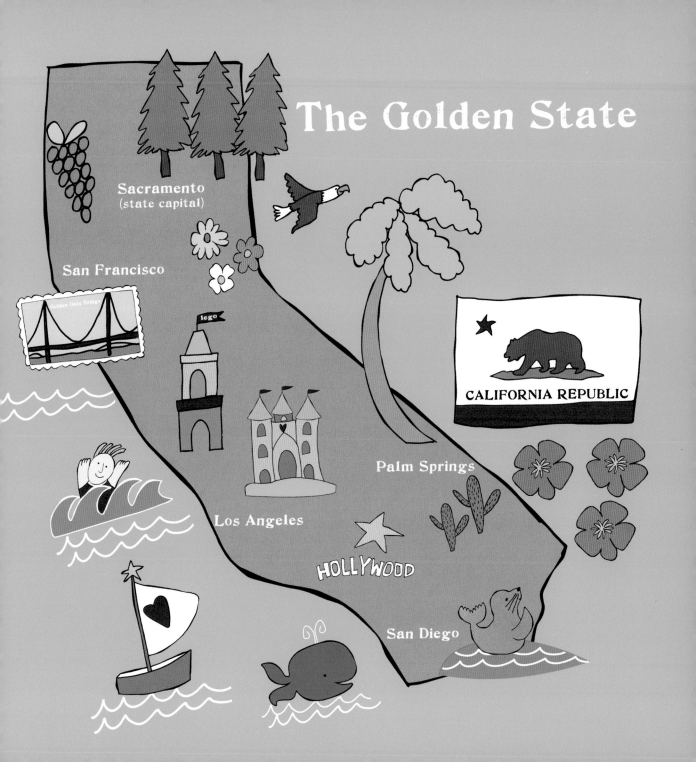

A is for awesome

because that's what California is in every way!

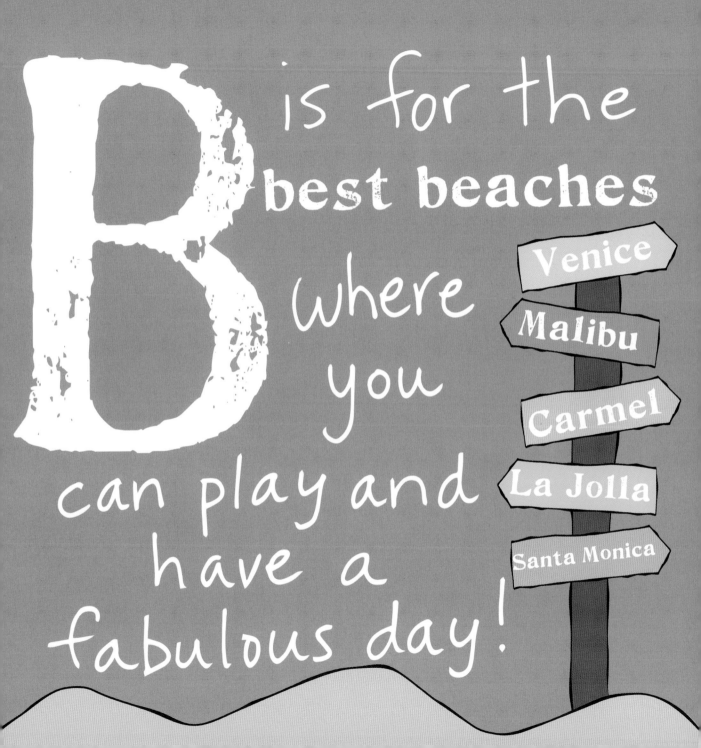

B is for the best beaches where you can play and have a fabulous day!

Venice

Malibu

Carmel

La Jolla

Santa Monica

C is for **cool** trees like the sequoia and redwood.

D

is for **Disneyland.**

Haven't been yet? You should!

E is for the bald **eagles** found soaring through the sky at Joshua Tree.

F
is for the wild flowers

from the Sierra Nevada to the sea.

G
is for the Golden Gate Bridge, one of our most favorite things.

Golden Gate Bridge

H is for ★ Hollywood,

where actors play chiefs, cowgirls and kings.

HOLLYWOOD

I is for what the **incredible** Monterey Bay Aquarium can teach.

J is for **jumping** through all the big, tall, cool, gnarly waves at Laguna Beach.

K is for the **kites** flown in Santa Barbara above the sand.

L is for a great day spent at the fantastic **Legoland.**

M is for the **monarch** butterflies that magically flutter and fill the air.

N is for nuts,

like sweet almonds and pistachios, that grow everywhere.

O is for **Oakland A's** baseball on a hot summer day.

Athletics

R is for the Rose Parade, fun from morning to night.

we love **Pasadena**

S is for sailing off Catalina on a windy day.

T is for
a **trip**

to
Palm Springs
to see a green
cactus sway.

U is for Unicorns.

the golden state

In California magic and wonder are always made.

V is for the violins at the Los Angeles Philharmonic being played.

W is for **whale watching** at Newport Beach, an experience to share.

X is for the

XOXO

Californians love to spread everywhere.

Y is for the beautiful Yosemite National Park.

Z is for the
ZOO
where grey
sea lions
swim around
and
bark.

San Diego
Zoo

And now our big
has come to
but you
back to
begin

adventure an end,
can go
A and
again!

Sandra Magsamen is a best-selling and award-winning artist, author, and designer whose meaningful and message-driven art has touched millions of lives, one heart at a time. She loves to travel and has had many awesome adventures around the world. For now, she lives happily and artfully in Vermont with her family and their dog, Olive.

A big thank you to my amazing studio team of Hannah Barry and Karen Botti. Their creativity, research tenacity and spirit of adventure have been invaluable as we crafted the ABC adventure series.

Sandra Magsamen

Text and illustrations © 2015 Hanny Girl Productions, Inc. www.sandramagsamen.com
Exclusively represented by Mixed Media Group, Inc. NY, NY.
Cover and internal design © 2015 by Sandra Magsamen

Published by Sourcebooks Jabberwocky, an imprint of Sourcebooks, Inc.
P.O. Box 4410, Naperville, Illinois 60567-4410
(630) 961-3900
Fax: (630) 961-2168
www.sourcebooks.com

Library of Congress Cataloging-in-Publication data is on file with the publisher.

Source of Production: Leo Paper, Heshan City, Guangdong Province, China
Date of Production: July 2015
Run Number: 5004063

Printed and bound in China.
LEO 10 9 8 7 6 5 4 3 2 1

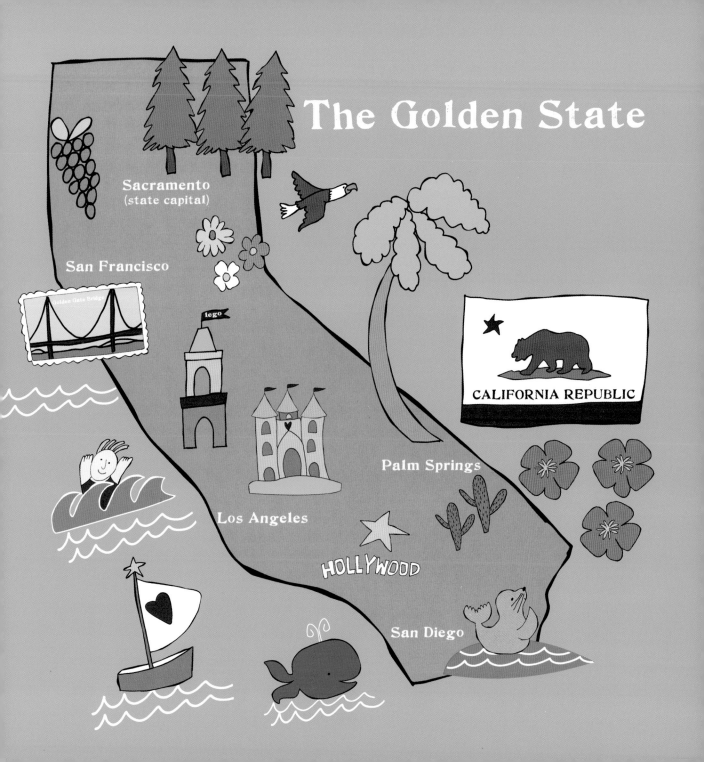

ABCDE
LMNOP
VWXYZ
FGHIJK